Make good choices.

Dana Lehman

I DOUBLE Dare You!

Written by Dana Lehman • Illustrations by Judy Lehman

Lehman Publishing
ALLENTON, MICHIGAN

Published by Lehman Publishing
15997 Hough Road
Allenton, Michigan 48002
www.lehmanpublishing.com

Edited by Imogene Zimmermann & Tina Hall (www.draftwords.com)
Design Layout by Gayle Brohl

Library of Congress Control Number: 2007908981
ISBN-13: 978-0-9792686-5-6
ISBN-10: 0-9792686-5-6

Acknowledgments

I would like to thank everyone that helped me with this book: Alice and Frank, for always giving their honest opinion. It was greatly needed and very much appreciated. I want to thank both of my editors, Tina, and Imogene, for their patience and expert advice. Gayle always does a fantastic job. The list of everything she has helped me with is too long to include. She is a great friend who continually supports and encourages me to move forward. Judy surpassed my expectations once again with her beautiful illustrations. I am thankful for having such a talented and dedicated mother-in-law. Of course, I have to thank my husband, Brian, and our two sons, Danny and Joey. They continually support me and inspire me to write new stories. Finally, I want to thank all my family and friends for all the encouragement they gave me to continue on this amazing journey.

Dana Lehman

I would like to thank my family for their continued support of my love for art. I am delighted to make these special animal friends found in Dana's book come alive on the pages to teach children valuable lessons. Each stroke with the brush makes a difference, just like each act we do in life. May we all learn to make the most of every day that we are given.

Judy Lehman

Walnut Grove was a wonderful place
to spend summer vacation.
Sammy was thrilled that his cousins,
Silly and Sassy, were coming for a visit.
Sammy's friends Rocky, a raccoon, and Bucky,
a beaver, were excited to meet his cousins.

Sammy's raccoon eyes always
reminded his friends that he was special,
so they expected his cousins
to be special, too.

Stories
about
Silly and
Sassy

Sammy loved his cousins,
but they *always* seemed to get into trouble.
Sammy was going to make sure
they did not create any problems.
Silly and Sassy were visiting Walnut Grove
for only one week.

After all,
how much trouble could
two little squirrels possibly
get into in seven days?
Sammy was about to
find out…

Now Open!
Deep Trouble Trail
and
Deep Water Bridge

Sammy decided
the best way to show
Silly and Sassy around
was to go on a hike
in the woods.
On their way to
Deep Trouble Trail,
they met Sammy's friends,
Rocky and Bucky.

As they entered the trail,
Sassy yelled,
"Let's play hide 'n seek.
You're it, Sammy!"

Sammy found Bucky right away.
He was hiding in a log.
Rocky climbed a tree to hide from Sammy,
but he fell out of the tree and landed
in a big pile of leaves.
Sammy still had to find Silly and Sassy.
He hoped they were not in trouble already…

Silly and Sassy were easily distracted.

They had already found another game to play.
Silly saw some big sticks that fell from the tree Rocky
climbed and said, "Sassy, I *dare* you to play swords
with me." Sassy remembered her mom telling them not
to play swords because someone could get hurt, but
she could not turn down a dare.

Sammy had taken his eyes off them
for only a couple of minutes,
but that was all it took for them to get into trouble.
Sammy looked everywhere for Silly and Sassy.
He finally found them playing swords
behind some pine trees.
Sammy approached them as Silly screamed,
"Sassy, you poked my eye!"

"Why were you playing swords?" asked Sammy.
"You both knew that you could get hurt."
Sassy answered, "It's Silly's fault I poked his eye.
He dared me to play swords!"
Sammy replied, "Sassy, you cannot blame Silly
for something you did.
You could have said NO!
You have to take responsibility
for your own actions."

Sassy felt terrible
about hurting Silly
and responded,
"I'm sorry
for poking
your eye, Silly.
I didn't do it on purpose."
Silly said, "I'm sorry too, Sassy.
I was wrong to dare you to play swords with me,
but I knew you couldn't turn down a dare."
Sammy said, "Let's go find Bucky and Rocky
so that we can find another game to play!"

They caught up with everyone by Paradise Pond.
Rocky and Bucky were having frog races.
Rocky yelled, "Find a frog in the pond;
    then come and play with us!"
They all went in search of the biggest,
    fastest frog that they could find.

Sassy walked down to the pond,
flipped over a rock,
and was surprised at what she found.
She screamed, "Yuck, a snake!"
She was so scared she fell into Paradise Pond.
Sammy helped her out of the water and said,
"Sassy, that is just a garter snake.
It won't hurt you."

Everyone was so busy watching Sassy;
they did not notice Silly and Bucky
climbing up Deep Water Bridge.
Sammy was the first to notice them and yelled,
"Silly! Bucky! Get down from there!
Someone is going to get hurt!"
But they were too far away to hear
Sammy's warning.

Bucky and Silly were standing at the edge
of the bridge looking down at Paradise Pond.
Bucky said, "It's a long way to the bottom."

Silly cheerfully replied,
"Yeah, it is, and I'm going for a swim!
I *dare* you to jump with me!"
Bucky considered jumping and then said,
"I don't know… I can't swim very well."

Silly didn't even hear Bucky's response.
Silly had already jumped in.
He was a good swimmer, but the jump was very high.

When Bucky looked down,
Silly was already swimming to shore.
Silly shouted, "Come on, Bucky!
I *double* dare you to jump!"

Bucky jumped…

It was a good thing
that Bucky's dad, Woody,
was watching everything.

After Bucky jumped in the water,
he had difficulty swimming back to shore.
He screamed, "Help! Help me!"

Just as Bucky went under the water,
Woody swam up and grabbed him.
All the animals stood and watched in disbelief.

Woody helped him safely back to shore,
then asked, "Bucky, can you tell me what happened?"
Bucky responded, "Silly *double* dared me to jump in,
so I had to do it! It's his fault I jumped!"

Woody thought carefully before replying,
"Just because someone dares you to jump off a bridge
doesn't mean that you jump off the bridge.
You have to take responsibility for your own actions.
You should have said **NO!**
You knew that you could get hurt!"

Silly felt awful that he had dared Bucky to jump
and said, "Bucky, I didn't know
that you couldn't swim very well.

I'm sorry; I thought that jumping off a bridge
would be fun.
I should have thought about our safety.
I am not going to dare anyone
to do anything anymore."

Sammy and his cousins
were happy that Bucky was not seriously hurt.
At least today,
everyone had learned a couple of valuable lessons.
It is important to take responsibility
for your own actions.
Sometimes that may be difficult.

Silly, Sassy, and Bucky have learned
not to blame anyone for their mistakes.
They learn from them and apologize
when they are wrong.
Hopefully in the future,
everyone
will remember
to think *before* they act.

Sammy
cannot believe
that Silly and Sassy
have been in
Walnut Grove
for only one day.
How much *more* trouble
could they possibly get into?

Only time will tell...

Deep
Trouble
Trail

Do you think Silly and Sassy should have been playing swords with their sticks?

Why did Sassy tell Silly that it was his fault that she had poked his eye?

Have you ever had frog races like Sammy and his friends? Did your frog win or lose? Did you have fun?

Why do you think that Sammy tried warning Silly and Bucky when they were climbing Deep Water Bridge? Have you ever warned your friends that they were going to get hurt doing something? Did they listen to you or do it anyway?

Have you ever played the game dare or double dare? What are some things that you have dared or been dared to do?

Why do you think that Bucky jumped off Deep Water Bridge? Would you do something knowing that you may get hurt?

Why do you think Bucky blamed Silly for having a difficult time swimming? Do you think that it is Silly's fault that Bucky had difficulty swimming back to shore?

What lessons do you think that Silly, Sassy, and Bucky have learned in Walnut Grove?

A Word from the Author

Sometimes people do things that they know they should not do. Many times, people make the wrong choice because they are following their friends. If you are not sure whether you should be doing something, ask yourself this question: would my mom or dad think that this is okay? This question might help you decide if your choice is right or wrong. Always do the right thing; do not do something just because your friends are. If you do make the wrong decision (and we all do sometimes), you have to take responsibility for your actions. No one can make you do anything. Do not blame anyone for the things that you do. Learn from your mistakes and think about what you could have done differently. Do not forget to apologize when you are wrong. You will have to make many choices in your life. Try to make them wisely. Remember good friends will support you when you make the right decisions, even if your decision is not the popular one.

I DOUBLE Dare You! is the second book in the Walnut Grove Series. All books in this series deal with character development. *I DOUBLE Dare You!* is a silver recipient of the Mom's Choice Award for developing social skills. The first book in this series, *Adventures at Walnut Grove: A Lesson about Teasing,* is a story about friends that learn to treat others as they would like to be treated. *Adventures at Walnut Grove* is also a silver recipient of the Mom's Choice Award for values and life lessons. The third book in this series, I CAN DO IT, helps children realize that with confidence, persistence, and determination, they can achieve their goals.

Dana resides in Allenton, Michigan, with her husband and their two children. Her children and love of nature continually inspire her to keep writing children's books.

Dana's mother-in-law, Judy Lehman, is her illustrator. Judy Lehman has been an artist and teacher for over forty years; she is a retired elementary school teacher. She currently resides in Hubbard Lake, Michigan, with her husband.

For more information on these books, including free lesson plans, please visit www.lehmanpublishing.com